JUST BE YOURSELF

By Eleanor Robins

Development: Kent Publishing Services, Inc.
Design and Production: Signature Design Group, Inc.
Illustrations: Jan Naimo Jones

SADDLEBACK PUBLISHING, INC.
Three Watson
Irvine, CA 92618-2767

Website: www.sdlback.com

ISBN 1-56254-772-0

Printed in the United States of America

1 2 3 4 5 6 08 07 06 05 04

Chapter 1

Rick was in the kitchen. His mom and dad were there too. Rick was tired. He hadn't slept well.

It was the first day of his senior year. Rick was glad to be a senior. But it was also his first day at Carter High. And he was worried about going to a new school.

His mom said, "Don't worry, Rick. I am sure you will like Carter High."

How could his mom be so sure? She had been to Carter High only once. And that was to sign him up for school.

His dad said, "Your mom is right, Rick. I am sure you will like Carter High."

But his dad hadn't been there at all.

His dad said, "Soon you will have many friends."

Maybe he would. But they might find out about his hearing problem. And they wouldn't want to be his friends then.

His dad said, "Let me know when you are ready to go. I will drive you to school."

"That's OK. I want to walk," Rick said.

Rick wasn't in a hurry to get to school. And it might do him good to walk.

Rick ate his breakfast. Then he got up to go.

He said, "I will see you after school."

His mom said, "Wait, Rick. Don't forget your hearing aid."

"Yes, Rick. Don't forget your hearing aid," his dad said.

"I am not going to wear it," Rick said.

He knew his mom and dad wouldn't like that. But it was his choice.

His dad said, "You have to wear it. You know you hear better when you do."

Rick said, "I don't care. I am not going to wear it."

His dad said, "You know you need to wear it, Rick. You make better grades when you do."

Rick knew that was true. He did make better grades when he wore it.

But he didn't want the teachers to know he didn't hear well. And he didn't want the students to know either.

Rick was good at lip reading. He did OK when he could see the people who were talking. At least most of the time he did OK.

His mom said, "You have to wear your hearing aid, Rick."

"I am not going to wear it," Rick said.

He was tired of arguing with his mom and dad.

"But why?" his mom asked.

Rick said, "You know why. I don't want the other students to know I have a hearing problem."

His dad said, "You are being silly, Rick. The other students won't care."

"But they will care. And I know what they will say about me," Rick said.

Some students at Rick's other school had made fun of him.

His dad said, "Just be yourself, Rick. Pretending you don't have a hearing problem isn't worth it. There are times when you should care what others say. But this isn't one of them."

That was easy for his dad to say. He wasn't the one who had to wear a hearing aid. And he wasn't the one the kids had made fun of.

Rick hurried out the door. What a way to start the first day of his senior year.

He had upset both his dad and his mom. And now they would worry about him too.

Chapter 2

Rick walked slowly to school. He saw a box just inside the door. It had maps of the school in it. He got one.

Rick knew he had Mrs. Dodd for his first class. But he didn't know where her room was. He tried to find it on the map.

A boy came in the school. He got a map too.

The boy said, "Hi. My name is Ed. I haven't seen you before. Are you new here?"

"Yeah," Rick said.

"I was new last year. So I know how hard the first day is. Do you need any help?" Ed asked.

"Yeah. I am trying to find Mrs. Dodd's room. I have her for my first class," Rick said.

Ed said, "I don't know who she is. She must be new. What class do you have her for?"

"History," Rick said.

Ed looked at his map. And Rick looked at his map.

Then Ed said, "I see her room. I am going that way. Do you want me to show you where it is?"

"Yeah. Thanks," Rick said.

"I am in a hurry to get to my class. So is it OK for us to walk fast?" Ed asked.

"Sure," Rick said.

Ed quickly walked Rick to his class.

Then Ed said, "Do you know who your other teachers are?"

Rick said, "No. The woman in the office said Mrs. Dodd would tell me."

"Do you want me to meet you here after our first class? Then I can show you where your next class is," Ed said.

"Thanks. That would be great," Rick said.

"OK. See you then," Ed said.

Ed quickly walked off.

Rick liked Ed. And he hoped he had made a friend.

Rick went in his class. He sat down at a desk in the front row. He liked to sit in the front row. That way he could hear the teacher.

The class was OK. But Mrs. Dodd gave them a lot of homework. And she said they would have to write a paper.

Rick heard most of what Mrs. Dodd said. But he didn't hear all of it.

The end of class bell rang. Ed was in the hall. He was waiting for Rick.

"Who do you have next?" Ed asked.

"Mrs. Vance for English," Rick said.

Ed said, "So do I."

The boys started to walk to class.

Ed looked at Rick. He asked, "How is your day going?"

"OK," Rick said.

The boys got to class. They went in. Ed sat down in the front row. And Rick sat down next to him.

They had a few minutes to talk.

Ed asked, "Who are your other teachers?"

Rick told him.

Ed said, "I don't have any more classes with you. When do you have lunch?"

Rick told him.

"I have lunch at the same time. Do you want to eat with me today?" Ed asked.

"Yeah. That would be great," Rick said.

Ed got up to leave. He seemed very nice. Rick liked him a lot. And he thought Ed wanted to be his friend.

Maybe he would like being at Carter High after all.

Chapter 3

A cute girl came into English class. She smiled at Rick. And Rick smiled at her. He wished he knew who she was.

Maybe Ed knew her. But it was time for class to start. So he couldn't ask Ed about her.

The English class was OK. But Mrs. Vance said they would have to write many papers. But at least they would be short papers.

Rick had math next. And that class was OK too.

Rick heard most of what the teachers said. But he didn't hear all of what they said.

It was time for lunch. Rick was

ready to eat. He hurried to the lunchroom.

Ed waited outside the lunchroom door for Rick.

Ed asked, "How is your day going so far?"

Rick said, "OK. But the teachers gave me a lot of homework."

"So did my teachers," Ed said.

The boys went in the lunchroom. They quickly got their lunch trays.

Then they went to a table and sat down.

Rick sat across from Ed. That way he could read Ed's lips.

The boys ate for a few minutes. Then Rick looked around the lunchroom. He saw the cute girl in his English class. She sat at a table near him.

Rick asked, "Do you know that girl over there?"

"Which one?" Ed asked.

Rick told him.

"Yes. I know her. Her name is Gail. She was new last year," Ed said.

"Does she have a boyfriend?" Rick asked.

"I don't think she does. But I don't know for sure. Do you want me to find out for you?" Ed asked.

"Yeah. Thanks," Rick said.

Ed said, "I will ask my girlfriend, Deb. She and Gail are friends. So she should know who Gail dates."

"Great. Thanks," Rick said.

Ed was nice. Rick was glad he had met Ed.

Gail looked over at them. She smiled at them and waved. Rick smiled at her and waved back.

"Do you want to meet her?" Ed asked.

"Yeah," Rick said.

"Eat fast. Then we will go over to her table, and you can meet her," Ed said.

"Great. Thanks," Rick said.

The boys quickly ate the rest of their lunches. They put their trays up. Then they walked over to Gail's table.

Ed told the girls that Rick was new to the school. Then he told Rick who the four girls were.

Rick said hi to all of the girls. But he didn't hear their names.

Then Ed said, "Rick is in our English class, Gail."

"I know. I saw him," Gail said.

Then she smiled at Rick again.

Gail said, "I hope you like Carter High, Rick."

Now that he had met Gail, Rick was sure he would like Carter High.

Rick had science after lunch. Gail was in the class too. Rick was glad about that. She smiled at him and waved.

Rick saw Ed after class was over.

Ed said, "I asked Deb about Gail for you. She said Gail doesn't have a boyfriend right now."

"Great. Thanks for finding out for me," Rick said.

"Are you going to ask her out?" Ed asked.

"I want to. But I don't know," Rick said.

Maybe he should be at the school longer before he asked a girl out.

Ed said, "You better ask Gail soon, before she starts to date someone else."

Maybe Ed was right. Maybe he should ask Gail out soon.

Chapter 4

The first week was OK for Rick. The work was not too hard. And his teachers were OK.

He ate lunch with Ed all week. And Rick was sure he had made a friend.

Gail was in two of his classes. And she smiled and waved at him all week. So Rick thought she liked him.

Only one thing was wrong. Rick heard most of what his teachers said. But he didn't hear all of it.

He worked on schoolwork most of the weekend. And he didn't ask Gail for a date.

It was the next Monday. Rick was on his way in the school.

Ed called to him. He said, "Rick, wait up. I will walk with you."

But Rick didn't hear Ed.

Ed ran up to him.

"I yelled at you to wait. Why didn't you wait for me?" Ed asked.

Rick didn't hear him. But Rick wasn't going to tell Ed that.

Rick said, "I am in a hurry. I don't have time to wait."

Ed seemed surprised. He said, "I thought you didn't hear me. I didn't know you just didn't want to stop. I don't want to keep you."

Ed hurried off. And he didn't give Rick time to say any more.

Rick didn't want Ed to go. But Rick couldn't ask him to come back. Then Ed would think Rick wasn't in a hurry. And he would think Rick had lied to him.

Rick hoped Ed wasn't mad at him.

He could tell Ed that he didn't hear him call out. But then Ed would know he had a hearing problem. And then Ed might not want to be his friend.

Rick went to his locker. He got his history book. It wasn't time for school to start. So he walked slowly to his class.

Ed came up to him.

Ed asked, "Do you have a few minutes now?"

"Sure," Rick said.

He was glad Ed wasn't mad at him.

"Have you asked Gail for a date yet?" Ed asked.

Rick said, "Not yet. But I might ask her to go to a movie."

"That sounds good," Ed said.

Some boys came up behind them. The boys were talking very loudly.

Ed looked at the boys. He wasn't looking at Rick.

Ed asked, "How would you like to doubledate with Deb and me? We could all go to a movie together."

There was too much noise in the hall. So Rick couldn't hear what Ed said.

Ed looked back at Rick. He asked, "So what do you say? Do you want to do that?"

Rick still didn't want Ed to know he had a hearing problem. So Rick didn't want to ask Ed what he just said.

So Rick said, "I don't know. I will have to think about it."

Ed seemed surprised.

He said, "OK."

Then Ed hurried down the hall. And he left Rick to walk by himself.

Rick wished he knew what Ed had asked him. And he hoped Ed wasn't mad at him.

Rick was glad when his first class was over. He was in a hurry to get to his English class. He wanted to see Ed.

Rick got to class before Ed did. He went to his desk and sat down.

Gail came in.

Gail said, "Hi, Rick."

"Hi," Rick said.

Ed came in. He sat down at the desk next to Rick. But he didn't say anything to Rick.

Or at least Rick didn't think he did.

Ed left as soon as the class was over. And he didn't ask Rick to walk with him.

Rick didn't see Ed again until lunch time. But Ed wasn't waiting for him by the lunchroom door. Ed was already inside.

Ed was eating with someone else. And he didn't ask Rick to join them.

So Rick ate by himself.

Chapter 5

It was the next day. Rick was in English class.

Mrs. Vance said, "Today we will talk about your first paper. You will need to turn it in next Monday."

"What do you want us to write about?" Ed asked.

Mrs. Vance said, "That is up to you this time. You can write about anything you like."

Rick was glad to hear that.

Mrs. Vance said, "But be sure to do a good job on it. You will get a grade on it."

"How long should it be?" Ed asked.

Mrs. Vance said, "It should be exactly two pages long. And make sure it isn't almost two pages long."

Some of the class laughed.

Rick was glad it wouldn't be a long paper.

He didn't know what to write about. But he was sure he would think of something. He would have to work on his paper over the weekend. So he couldn't ask Gail for a date.

Soon the class was over. Rick went out in the hall. He started to go to his next class.

Gail walked behind him.

Gail said, "Wait, Rick. I will walk with you."

But some students were talking near Rick. And he didn't hear Gail. So Rick didn't wait for Gail.

The next two days went by slowly for Rick.

Ed was nice to Rick in class. But he didn't walk to class with Rick. And he didn't eat lunch with Rick either.

Rick thought Ed must be upset with him. Was it because he didn't hear what Ed said to him on Monday? Rick wished he knew what Ed said. But he wouldn't ask Ed to tell him.

Gail still smiled at him. But not as much as before.

And he couldn't hear all of what the teachers said.

It was Friday. Rick was in English class. It was almost time for class to start.

Rick looked over at Ed.

He said, "I have to write my paper this weekend. Have you written your paper yet?"

"Yes. I wrote it last night," Ed said.

Rick didn't think Ed was going to say any more.

But then Ed said, "Be sure to check your spelling. Some teachers take points off for poor spelling. And Mrs. Vance might too."

"Thanks for telling me," Rick said.

Maybe Ed wasn't upset with him after all.

Rick hoped Ed would eat lunch with him. But Ed didn't eat with Rick.

Rick wrote his paper over the weekend. He tried to do the best he could. He hoped Mrs. Vance would think he did a good job.

Chapter 6

It was the next week. Rick was in English class.

Mrs. Vance said, "I graded your papers. Most of you did well. But some of you should have worked harder. You are seniors this year. And you should do better work than this."

Mrs. Vance passed out the papers. Rick could hardly wait to see his grade. He hoped he did well.

Mrs. Vance gave Rick his paper. She said, "Good job, Rick."

Rick quickly looked at his paper. He got an A.

Mrs. Vance passed out the rest of the

papers. Then she walked to the chalkboard.

She started to write on the board. She had her back to the class. And Rick couldn't read her lips.

Mrs. Vance said, "Rick had a very good paper. Tell the class about it, Rick."

Rick didn't hear Mrs. Vance. So he didn't say anything.

Mrs. Vance stopped writing on the board. She turned around. And she looked at Rick.

Mrs. Vance asked, "Why didn't you tell the class, Rick?"

Rick couldn't tell the class. He didn't know what Mrs. Vance wanted him to say.

"Well, Rick. Why didn't you tell the class? Didn't you hear me?" Mrs. Vance asked.

Rick could tell Mrs. Vance he didn't hear her. But he didn't want Mrs. Vance to know he had a hearing problem. And he didn't want his class to know either.

So he didn't tell Mrs. Vance anything.

Rick just said, "Yeah. I heard you. I just didn't want to tell the class."

Rick knew he sounded mad. But he couldn't help it. He didn't like it when someone thought he didn't hear well.

Mrs. Vance seemed very surprised.

Rick was sorry he had been rude to Mrs. Vance. He liked Mrs. Vance. And he wanted her to like him too.

Mrs. Vance said, "Stay after class, Rick. We will talk about this."

But Rick didn't know what they were going to talk about. He only knew he was in trouble. Maybe it was because he didn't hear well.

Some of the students told the class about their papers. And then it was time for class to be over.

Gail walked by Rick's desk. But she didn't look at him. And she didn't say anything to him.

The other students left. It was Mrs. Vance's planning time. So it was just Mrs. Vance and Rick.

Mrs. Vance said, "I am sorry about what happened, Rick. I didn't mean to upset you."

That surprised Rick.

Mrs. Vance said, "Your paper was very good. And I thought you would want to tell the class about it."

So that was what Mrs. Vance wanted him to do. Rick wished he had known that. He was proud of his paper. And he would like to tell the class about it.

"Some students don't like to share their work with the class. And that is OK with me, Rick. I won't ask you to do that again," Mrs. Vance said.

"I am sorry I was rude to you, Mrs. Vance. And I would like to tell the class about my paper. Do you want me to do that tomorrow?" Rick asked.

Mrs. Vance seemed very surprised. She said, "That would be fine, Rick."

Mrs. Vance seemed as if she wanted to ask Rick why he changed his mind.

Mrs. Vance said, "You can tell the class about your paper first thing tomorrow. Now I will write you a late pass. You might be late to your next class."

Mrs. Vance quickly wrote a late pass. She gave it to Rick.

Then she said, "Have a good day, Rick. I will see you tomorrow."

Rick quickly left. He was glad Mrs. Vance didn't seem mad at him.

He almost told Mrs. Vance about his hearing problem. But he still didn't want anyone at school to know about it.

Chapter 7

Things weren't going well for Rick. He wished he had never come to Carter High.

Rick had told the English class about his paper. And that was OK. But he got back tests in history and in math. Rick hadn't done well on them. And he knew why. He had heard only some of what the teachers had said.

Rick was on his way to lunch. He knew he would have to eat by himself. And he didn't like to do that. Rick wanted to eat with Ed. But Ed didn't seem to want to eat with him.

Was Ed mad at him? Rick had to know. But he didn't want to ask Ed in class.

Rick went in the lunchroom. He saw Ed. Ed sat at a table by himself.

Rick quickly got his lunch. He walked over to Ed's table.

He asked, "OK for me to sit here?"

Ed seemed surprised. He said, "Sure. Sit down."

Rick sat down across from Ed so he could read Ed's lips.

Rick asked, "Are you mad at me, Ed?"

Ed was surprised. He said, "No. Why would I be?"

Rick said, "You stopped walking to class with me. And you stopped eating with me too. So I thought you might be mad at me."

At first Ed didn't say anything.

But then he said, "I am not mad at you, Rick. I just thought you didn't want to be friends with me. So I didn't think you wanted to walk to class or eat lunch with me."

Rick asked, "Why? Is it because I didn't stop when you called to me?"

Ed said, "It isn't just that. I thought I might be wrong about that. But later I asked you to doubledate with Deb and me. And you said you didn't know if you wanted to do it. Then you didn't say any more about it. So I was sure you didn't want to be friends."

Rick was very surprised. He said, "But I would like to doubledate with you. I just didn't hear you ask me."

Ed seemed very surprised. He said, "You must have. You answered me."

Rick didn't want to tell Ed the truth. But he knew he had to tell him. It might be too late to be Ed's friend. But he didn't want Ed to think he didn't like him.

Rick said, "I knew you had said something. But I didn't know what. And I didn't want to ask you. I didn't want you to know that I have a hearing problem."

Ed asked, "You do? So why didn't you just tell me that?"

"I thought you wouldn't want to be my friend," Rick said.

Ed asked, "Why? Do you think I wouldn't like you because you have a hearing problem?"

"Yeah," Rick said.

"Why would you think that? I care only about what kind of person you are, not what kind of problems you have. We all have problems," Ed said.

Rick had never thought about it that way before.

Ed asked, "Is that why you were

rude to Mrs. Vance? Didn't you hear what she asked you to do?"

"Yeah," Rick said.

"Have you ever had a hearing aid?" Ed asked.

"Yeah," Rick said.

"Why don't you wear it? Doesn't it help you?" Ed asked.

"Yeah," Rick said. It helped him a lot.

"So why don't you wear it?" Ed asked.

"I don't want people to know I need one," Rick said.

Ed said, "I am not trying to be rude, Rick. But that is silly. What is the big deal about wearing a hearing aid? Some people wear glasses to see better. So why not wear a hearing aid to hear better?"

"But some people might not like me

because I wear a hearing aid," Rick said.

"That is their problem, Rick. It's not yours," Ed said.

Ed was right. That was their problem. It wasn't his problem. Why did it take him so long to know that?

And Rick didn't need a person like that for a friend. He didn't need a person like that for a girlfriend either.

He would start wearing his hearing aid. And people could like him or not. That was up to them.

But Rick knew one thing for sure. He would be able to hear well.

Chapter 8

Lunch time was over. Rick and Ed left the lunchroom. Gail was in the hall. She was walking by herself.

Rick looked over at Ed. He asked, "Do you still want to doubledate with me?"

Ed said, "Sure. How about next Friday night?"

"Great. I will ask Gail now," Rick said.

He was going to tell Gail about his hearing problem. He didn't know how she would feel about it. So he wasn't sure she would date him. But he might as well find out now.

Rick called to her. He said, "Gail, wait."

Gail stopped. She turned around. And she waited for Rick.

"Is it OK for me to walk to class with you?" he asked.

At first Gail didn't answer. She looked as if she didn't want to walk with him.

Then she said, "I don't want to be rude to you, Rick. But I don't want to walk to class with you."

"Why?" he asked.

Had she found out about his hearing problem?

But how could she have known? Ed was the only one who knew about it. And Ed hadn't told her.

"I asked you to walk to class with me one day, Rick. But you didn't wait for me. I thought you didn't hear me. But now I know you are just rude," Gail said.

Rick didn't know Gail had asked him to do that. So that surprised him very much.

Gail said, "I thought you were nice. And I liked you. But now I am not sure you are nice. You were very rude to Mrs. Vance. And I don't like boys who are rude. So I don't want to walk with you."

"But I am not really like that," Rick said.

Gail seemed as if she didn't believe him.

She asked, "Then why do you act that way?"

Rick said, "I didn't hear you. That is why I didn't walk with you. And I didn't hear Mrs. Vance either. So I didn't know what she wanted me to do."

Gail asked, "Why were you rude to

her? Why didn't you just tell her you didn't hear her?"

"I didn't want her to know. And I didn't want the class to know," Rick said.

"Why?" Gail asked.

"I have a hearing problem. And I don't want people to know about it. So I don't wear my hearing aid," Rick said.

Gail seemed very surprised.

She said, "So that is why you act rude sometimes."

"Yeah," Rick said.

Gail smiled at him. She said, "Then wear your hearing aid. That way you can hear Mrs. Vance, and you can hear me too. Now we need to stop talking and get to class. We will be late."

"One more thing," Rick said.

"What?" Gail asked.

"Will you go to a movie with me next Friday night? We can doubledate with Ed and Deb," Rick said.

"Sure. That sounds like fun," Gail said.

"Great," Rick said.

"Now we need to get to class," Gail said.

They hurried to class.

Rick felt very good. Ed didn't seem to care about his hearing problem. And Gail didn't seem to care about it either. So he didn't have to hide his hearing problem anymore.

Rick was glad he didn't have to pretend anymore. He could just be himself.

He was glad he came to Carter High. Rick was going to have a good senior year after all.